The Familiar

Poems

Sarah Kain Gutowski

Praise for *The Familiar*

"How well I know these forms of self-splitting, of self-reproach, of taking an endless self-inventory that only ever leads to recrimination and concern. I always think that I'm the only one who plays both parts in my head as I wonder why I'm not better, smarter, kinder, humbler, more generous—or simply put—why it feels like I'm never enough. I know I'm not the only one who will be grateful for Sarah Kain Gutowski's *The Familiar*. I know I'm not the only one who will feel less alone after reading these poems. I wish I could learn the lessons of wholeness this collection points the way towards, though I know I won't. But then again, I just might."

—Jason Schneiderman, author of *Hold Me Tight*

"Sarah Kain Gutowski's richly-detailed *The Familiar* is divided into selves: the ordinary and extraordinary. With ruthless scrutiny, Gutowski makes the reader aware of the enormous, invisible labor of women and its attendant exhaustion. The ordinary self holds the world together and the extraordinary self contains desire and ambition—desires that are almost impossible in the world of familial responsibility. Yet, in the end, the distinction between ordinary and extraordinary is not so clear. Gutowski leads the reader to an unexpected liberation that made me laugh out loud, a rare pleasure in poetry. *The Familiar* is brilliant, witty, and unafraid to relentlessly question the sacred territory of family responsibility."

—Jessica Cuello, author of *Liar* and *Yours, Creature*

"In *The Familiar*, Sarah Kain Gutowski takes the fragmentation of self to a whole new level. This fabulist poetic narrative of midlife crisis pits the Ordinary Self against the Extraordinary Self—one attuned to the daily mundanities of housekeeping and motherhood, the other hysterical with ambition and adventure—as warring factions of identity. 'We all house within our skin and brains,' Gutowski writes, 'another self or two, whole persons devoted to one aspect/ of twenty-first century life.' And it's not too long before 'shit hits the fan.' It's all here: domestic life, travel, sex, even attempted murder. Both deeply analytical and a wild ride, both elevated in lyric language and peppered with lowbrow quips, *The Familiar* resists parable and acknowledges the inevitably multifaceted nature of selfhood, what is expected of women, and what women expect of themselves. Fierce. Vulnerable. Entertaining."

—Cynthia Marie Hoffman, author of *Exploding Head*

"Sarah Kain Gutowski's *The Familiar* exists as part haunting, part conjuration, and part poetic experiment in which the intricacies and intimacies of a poet's intertwined selves are revealed in triplicate. Thank heavens, given such a daunting task, that the poet's 'inevitable self' possesses an existential wit and fortitude; these stanzas exude the grit of a 'Sartrean grandmother,' who supplants ego, and shadows this intriguing conceit, where extra and ordinary alternately lift off and land—at home in New York, inconspicuous in London, or even spontaneously in Italy. More than navigating shades of chaos and order, *The Familiar* is that rare collection that meta-captures the trajectories and disparate psyches necessary to the poetic mind. And these poems ordinarily feature extraordinary endings! Readers, you may just glimpse your selves' frugal, unreasonable, and even indomitable sheen in these dexterous tercets, where we're lucky enough to be surprised by ourselves, by the audacity of azaleas, by blandness (which is truly camouflage!), and by the wonders of the ordinary and everyday that keep us alive."

—Matt Schumacher, Managing Editor of *Phantom Drift: A Journal of New Fabulism*

Library of Congress Cataloging-in-Publication Data

Names: Gutowski, Sarah Kain, author.
Title: The familiar : poems / Sarah Kain Gutowski.
Description: First edition. | Huntsville : TRP: The University Press of SHSU, [2024]
Identifiers: LCCN 2023033054 (print) | LCCN 2023033055 (ebook) | ISBN 9781680033281 (paperback) | ISBN 9781680033298 (ebook)
Subjects: LCSH: Midlife crisis--Poetry. | Middle-aged women--Psychology--Poetry. | Identity (Psychology)--Poetry. | LCGFT: Poetry.
Classification: LCC PS3607.U85 F36 2024 (print) | LCC PS3607.U85 (ebook) | DDC 811/.6--dc23/eng/20230725
LC record available at https://lccn.loc.gov/2023033054
LC ebook record available at https://lccn.loc.gov/2023033055

FIRST EDITION

Front cover image courtesy: Sarah Kain Gutowski
Photos courtesy: Sarah Kain Gutowski

Cover design by Bradley Alan Ivey
Interior design by Bradley Alan Ivey

Printed and bound in the United States of America

TRP: The University Press of SHSU
Huntsville, Texas 77341
texasreviewpress.org

Table of Contents

"The boundary between the imaginary and the real is even less distinct in this troubled period than during puberty. One of the most salient characteristics in the aging woman is the depersonalization that makes her lose all objective landmarks. People in good health who have come close to death also say they have felt a curious impression of doubling; when one feels oneself to be consciousness, activity, and freedom, the passive object affected by fate seems necessarily like another: *I* am not the one run over by a car. *I* am not the old woman the mirror shows me."

—Simone de Beauvoir, *The Second Sex*

"We aren't here to make things perfect. The snowflakes are perfect. The stars are perfect. Not us. Not us! We are here to ruin ourselves and to break our hearts and love the wrong people and die. The storybooks are bullshit."

—Ronny Cammareri, *Moonstruck* (written by John Patrick Shanley, directed by Norman Jewison)

The Familiar

Poems

Sarah Kain Gutowski

TRP: The University Press of SHSU
Huntsville, Texas 77341

familiar
fuh-**mil**-yer

— noun

8. a familiar friend or associate
9. Also called **familiar spirit**. *Witchcraft and Demonology*. A supernatural spirit or demon, often in the form of an animal, supposed to serve and aid a witch or other individual.
10. *Roman Catholic Church*:
    a. an officer of the Inquisition, employed to arrest accused or suspected persons.
    b. a person who belongs to the household of the pope of or a bishop, rendering domestic though not menial service.

from Dictionary.com Unabridged,
based on the *Random House Unabridged Dictionary*

We Want for More

Among the garden's weeds my extraordinary self sits,
wondering how she came to this: banishment, but gradual—
an exile by degrees. One day, praise like sun in June; then

shadow: not so much reprisal as silence, stretched long
as overcast sky. Now, squatting near the mute watermelon
and cucumber hills, ornamental leaves that don't belong

catch her eye. She marvels at the weed's tenacity, how it
clings to the other plants, how much precision and time
it takes to remove tendrils of bad from good. Despite

the low clouds, my extraordinary self is a burnt mess,
and between the pain peeling her shoulders and soil
that coats her teeth, she cannot help but feel self-pity,

watching her image distort in the weed's gloss then
disappear when she removes the vine. It seems
a shame to waste such ambition, such determination,

but the purslane—flowering, delectable when consumed—
threatens the cultivated vegetables and fruit. It's beautiful,
but wrong for this patch of earth. She slices its roots

with her spade and scatters the knots and emerald stalks
and gorgeous vine into the compost heap. *Little sister,*
she thinks. *It's time to leave. We want for more than we should.*

A Great Damage

My ordinary self wakes but can't remember when
she fell asleep in this room: The sheets, slick with damp,
feel unfamiliar; grit rims her eyelids and even

the mattress feels foreign, like something loaned
from memory's recesses. We haven't seen her for years.
She hasn't been allowed to visit. Now she's here

suddenly, as if summoned by a spell, and welcomed—
coaxed and flattered by our pleas. Desperation's humidity
rises from the bed. Daylight, dishwashers, doctor's offices—

my ordinary self must become reacquainted
with ordinary living. She wanders the rooms. Her feet sink,
make light depressions in the carpet and brief, dark splotches

on the hard wood. She thinks about making an appointment
for an oil change. She consults the kitchen's calendar, but its
coded loops of pen and cross-outs confuse, refuse to clarify.

There's too much to undo here, she thinks. *A great damage*
has been done. Panic beads her skin. As if on cue
from our bedroom's shadows, the clock shrieks in alarm.

A Little Push

My extraordinary self turned out to be less extraordinary
than we'd anticipated. She wasn't even good at packing up
her things: she kept removing, then replacing, her tap shoes

and favorite sequined gowns—glitter escaping cellophane
to coat her fingers, the bedspread, all surfaces inside
and beyond her suitcase. Now we find reminders of her

everywhere. My ordinary self lifts the shades in the morning
and frowns—sunlight refracts off tiny squares adhered
to the nightstand, the hamper's wicker rings. This will take

hours and days to remove. Her personal items sit tossed
in a corner, what we found after she'd left: wads of foreign
paper currency; a camera leaking acrid batteries;

the loose ephemera of a brief photography career.
She left not in a rush but in a cloud of disarray and tears,
the melodrama that marked her too overwrought

for the stage. She didn't want to stay but didn't want
to go, didn't want to make the decision to separate.
My ordinary self gave her a little push: nothing too

vicious, just pressure along the shoulders that said: *This
is your direction.* It was the tree leaves grinding like teeth
that whispered: *It won't do any good to look back.*

Gooseflesh

If she'd been around for those missing years,
my ordinary self wonders, would our life now be this
sad collection? She surveys the disrepair and marvels

at the neglect: The splintered cabinetry. Scratched
floorboards. Sheetrock nails pushing ghostly thumbs
through thinning, spectral paint. She pulls open

the closet door, looses its demon: hot breath spews forth
coats and boots and mittens. *We need a priest, not a maid,*
she thinks. Down the road, inside a motel room

or the car she's made her home, my extraordinary self's
skin crawls with a flush of cold. Hairs stand on end
like someone walks—no, stomps—across her grave.

Naming

My ordinary self insists—from doctors, to teachers,
to butchers, to the crossing guard by the funeral home—
Names are so important. She has the children look up

everyday birds in the garden: Catbird. Grackle. Starling.
Together they create tags for the plants and shrubs:
Cyclamen. Hydrangea. Rose of Sharon. She even helps

the clerk identify herbs at checkout: *This, oregano. This,
sage.* She writes everything down. *Everyone prefers
the correct label to the wrong*, she says, *and most prefer*

a label even if they insist out loud they don't. My ordinary self,
for instance, takes pleasure from hers: Proficient. Able.
Steady. On her arm, tattooed in script: *uidelicet incorruptum*.

Time to Clean

She wasn't extraordinary, my extraordinary self,
for the measure of her accomplishments. Rather,
her visions were operatic, symphonic, and robust.

It was her effort's tenor, its deep vibrating notes
that made those plans appear unique. And yet
so much broken glass, so much mess in endeavor.

So many busted enamel shards, rusted cables,
antique lamps collecting dust. The unused spools
of twine, boxes of glue, parts for builds abandoned.

Piles of books, face-down and dog-eared,
then forgotten. So much everything
and so much nothing—enthusiasm multiplied

and left to molder in humid air: A warehouse
for unrealized dreams. Simply put, it was time
to clean. But it was difficult for her to let go:

We were crows chasing each other from the trees—
clarion in our anger. All around our home,
broken spider silk drifted in the breeze.

The Rational Optimist

The consummate wife, my ordinary self helps my husband
pack when he needs to leave on business, a checklist of items
in her back jeans pocket, her knack for rolling clothes

and using shoes for storage such a boon. When there's time
she leaves notes folded inside his shirt pockets, or tucked
within his cufflinks box. Such a difference from when

my extraordinary self would see him off—her petulant silence
a lock to which we'd all forgotten the combination. Sometimes
I think she hid his passport just to keep him home extra

minutes, each one tense as stand-by. How patient he was,
back then, to withstand this torture because he was leaving,
supporting his family; all the while his wife resentful,

her jealousy slender but sharp as a new moon. My ordinary self
is far more rational, and an optimist. Awakened for a pre-dawn
send-off, she kisses him softly, says she'll see him soon.

They Sing Her Praises

In something of a paradox, my ordinary self is rather
extraordinary. My ordinary self has follow-through.
Not all of the natural world—or the unnatural—has this

persistence, the dogged will to see a thing done
to its very damn end. That's why she's so good
at laundry. She remembers how important it is

to keep the clothes from pressing too far
into one another, creating canyons of wrinkles.
She avoids embarrassing piles of socks and thongs

and linens from forming new terrain on the furniture.
She hangs when delicates need drying, folds
when the cycle is finished. She itemizes by type,

material, color, and care. These days no one ever
goes without matching socks, unless by choice.
My ordinary self is tireless, albeit weary

of fitted sheets and their stubborn, imperfect corners.
In the basement laundry crickets keep her company.
They sing her praises in the dark, though no one listens.

Climate of Destruction

When she reenters the office, my ordinary self recognizes
signs of storm and stress, my extraordinary self's chaotic
occupancy. She flicks the computer on. It groans in protest,

slicks blue light across every object beneath the monitor's
patient face. She searches for the keyboard, but
a label maker's all she finds under last quarter's financials.

Piles of drop-and-run litter the desk: leather portfolios
crowded with legal pads, accordion files spilling receipts,
torn staples, chains of paper clips, pens without caps

buried like shallow land mines and blooming red wounds
across take-out napkins. Underneath the desk, where her feet
should rest, boxes of yellowed paper files decamp.

A cricket carcass dries to dust beside them. On the shelves
manilla folders buckle like a collapsed bridge beneath
stacks of books. She moves aside a dead plant and types

a memo: *To the occupant(s): Please remember the company
cannot sustain growth in a pervasive climate of destruction
and disorganization.* She hits Print. Across the hall

paper jams and another machine complains. She turns on
the overhead fluorescent lights. The whole room hums
with stark dissatisfaction. Her pupils shrink to pin pricks.

Dreaming and What-ifs

Overwhelmed by all she has been tasked to do,
my ordinary self calls a meeting. We sit down
and brainstorm a way to make her transition manageable.

We bullet-item lists and create spreadsheets. We draft
mission and vision statements and action plans, and when
our eyes begin to glaze, fingers cramped from note-taking,

my ordinary self stands and says, *All right. Let's get
to work.* This is crucial, this difference between my two
selves: my ordinary self's literal movement away

from the pens and pads of planning. She doesn't
mess around. Somewhere—not too far away, but removed
from here—at a similar table, my extraordinary self stares

at a lamp's glass bell as if she could read our future.
Yet she's naught but dreaming and what-ifs—under her,
so little came to fruition. She played us: all glad-handing

and misdirection, and wouldn't admit failure, even
when smoke alarms sounded and ash flitted through
the air like kitchen moths born from the stale and fetid.

Backseat Scores

It's not like we drew up charges and nailed them to the door.
One morning my ordinary self appeared—much older
of course, than we'd seen her last, yet still her essential

ordinary self. So dependable. So not extraordinary.
But the house couldn't hold us all—not enough
hot water, only so much space on the family couch.

My extraordinary self took it badly, jumped
fully clothed into denial. She made claims
about promises, sacrifice, and betrayal. Quite frankly,

it was embarrassing. My ordinary self moved
around her in a tidy silence, sweeping the broken dishes
off the floor. Then my extraordinary self

changed tactics: She took the children to a waterpark,
a carnival, and the arcade. Next, she bought
two sets of crotchless panties and took my husband

on long, indulgent car rides. She cooked elaborate meals.
And yet my dog liked my ordinary self more—
she never forgot to feed him—and the children ran to her

with their cuts and sores. Even my husband preferred
my ordinary self's predictable morning sex to roadside
backseat scores. My extraordinary self had to admit

defeat. My ordinary self would stay and she would leave.
That last night while the family watched *The Avengers*
she curled fetal on the carpet and wept noisily at our feet.

Daily Ghosts

My ordinary self must contend daily with the ghosts
of my extraordinary self, who wore so many names
in the past like fake moustaches or hats and coats

that hid her true form. My ordinary self hears the names
called in her direction. Someone thinks they've seen
my extraordinary self on the street, outside the salon

or the bait and tackle shop, and each time she must turn
so they can see her eyes, and so she can see their eyes,
too, and how they fall, weighted by disappointment

or embarrassment. *No,* this is not that woman, *you
were thinking of someone else.* The ghosts always appear
afterwards, when my ordinary self turns back and sees

her reflection in the glass storefront. Briefly, but dark
as the maple's shadow, my extraordinary self appears:
her hangdog look grotesque, like a false face worn

for a masque. Her lips move as if she speaks,
but my ordinary self hears only birdcall and trees rustling.
Then, like a leaf falling in wind, my extraordinary self

disappears. My ordinary self sees only her own face refracted
by the shop door glass. She takes a breath. Spots the clerk
and remembers to ask about fishing line and weighted lures.

We Were Complicit

We had long conversations about our extraordinary self
when we were younger. My ordinary self and I would dream
and concoct elaborate schemes for her while we lied

on our twin bed and listened to cicada song crawl
up the trees during hot, long, Virginia summers.
All the precocious toddler tales our mother told

were about her. In the third grade, she won a contest
with a dance routine half-improvised. She ghosted
completely in middle school—no surprise—

and then returned sophomore year, when she published
an exposé in the local paper. Even then, my ordinary self
held down the fort with grades solid but not flashy,

and stayed undetected by popular cliques and bullies alike.
She used to say that nothing could stop us. Under the helm
of our extraordinary self, our ship would come in.

Our star would ascend. A sad, mixed bag of metaphors,
we kept and groomed her, our extraordinary self,
like a pet—praised every correct action until

she felt she could do no wrong. So really, we were complicit.
We created our monster. My poor extraordinary self—
her smile so wide and stupid before the vanity,

so brave before the photographer's flash, yet always
rushing through her lines. And my ordinary self nothing
but a dusky shadow or prop dissolving into background.

Torn and Useless

Some mornings she rises and walks by the river, watching
the ducks and geese ignore each other; the mosquitos rise
in clouds above the humid bank and disperse with the breeze;

and dragonflies hover and couple and drop in a green, erratic
rhythm. She's had a difficult time knowing what
she should do with her days, my extraordinary self, since

she left our home. Other mornings she sits on the steps
of the library, tries to avoid staring at patients waiting
for methadone. Instead she watches the woman in slippers

and a crop top shuffle away from them all. A sour, pre-dawn
yeasty odor lingers around the bakery and she considers
eating. Usually, though, she forgoes the croissant or roll

and walks to Main Street, watching gridlock build
to an angry knot. She feels the drivers' tension fill her
empty stomach, their need and anxiety writ in the script

of their eyes. They squint against the sun's rising assault.
She remembers waking each morning with a cramp,
ambition enflaming her gut. Now she is calm and strangely

present, aware of everything she ignored before she moved
out of our home, but she feels murky and static all
the same—no less a zombie than the woman who drags

her scuffs against the warming asphalt, who tries now
to cross the teeming intersection in rush hour traffic,
the tracks on her arms the outline of a torn, useless map.

Recurring Catastrophes

My ordinary self is not great at networking.
Her conversation's void of art and humor, not
because she doesn't know what to say but rather

her dearth of interest. She won't respond to emails,
schedule dinner dates, return phone calls—all gestures
other ordinary people make to stay connected

and maintain relationships. My ordinary self runs
a little warm when asked about her lack of friends.
If I become distracted by other people and their

other problems, she once said, *how can I focus on ours?*
At this point in our life, she is correct—fires keep
erupting at home, and spread: to school, to work,

and on the flat, dry road to the grocery. Everywhere, smoke
and heat and the need to escape. My extraordinary self
is never around for these recurring catastrophes

but my ordinary self and I can feel her like the tremor
underfoot when a house folds its charred frame to the ground:
somewhere, she's smiling, her eyes hot and gray as ash.

Between Pleasure and Worry

My ordinary self abstains from vice so vacation is never
great when she's in charge. Granted, our trips are more
organized. Everyone remembers to bring a toothbrush.

The children have underwear, an appropriate amount
of socks. The car is packed tight as a high score in Tetris.
Consider, too, how leisure tastes strange and slightly bitter

to my extraordinary self's tongue: how she cannot truly
go on vacation without vacillating between pleasure—
ice cream dinners, salt-on-skin, ocean air threading

through one's clothes and hair—and worry, her anxiety
worn thick like sunscreen about whatever else she could be
or should be doing instead as part of a discombobulated,

oversized climb toward greatness. So while she may not be
the most imaginative—we visit the same parks, patronize
similar tchotchke shops, buy newer versions of neon shirts—

my ordinary self knows how to truly rest. We read books
for pleasure, take aimless walks. When the children ask,
what are we going to do today, her answer is always ready,

like a puzzle piece falling into place, easy because it belongs
in this one space: *We're going to have fun,* she answers. And this
really burns my extraordinary self: The children believe it.

A True Believer

My ordinary self reads magazines—commercial, not trade.
Specialization is a death sentence in this age, she likes to say.
Everyone needs to know a little bit about everything. She was,

back in college, a true believer in liberal arts: the one who
woke us up in time for History of Math, who kept our sorry
collective ass from failing geology lab, who made sure

in our junior and senior years we took at least one course
outside our chosen major. My extraordinary self was a student
arts reporter, founded an avant-garde literary magazine,

took extracurricular classes in performance and film.
She's kind of turning into an asshole, my ordinary self
would say back then, thumbing through fashion ads,

perched on our narrow twin bed. My extraordinary self,
her own head lost inside some art journal "conversation"
between composer and architect, would roll her eyes.

Foucault thinks you're the asshole. In the common room,
our suitemates watched sitcoms and soap operas, studied
for law exams. Outside the dorm someone's boyfriend

stumbled—drunk and high on forties, weed, Wittgenstein
and Kant—and fell face-first into the snow, passing into
a deep sleep just beyond our locked and frosted window.

To Feed and Stoke a Fire

There are shared interests, believe it or not. Both women,
for instance, love my husband equally, devotedly. He answers
questions they hold locked and kernelled in their hearts.

My ordinary self: attracted to his early morning rising,
ritual lovemaking, his homebody need to return from work
each evening and play with the dog, or tend to the yard while

the children ride their bikes. My extraordinary self loves
his bad-boy side, the one inclined to blow off work for a day
at the beach, the one willing to drop thousands for a trip

overseas. The get-drunk-and-fuck side. If my husband had
two selves, what a weird commune we'd be. Instead,
from her exile address, my extraordinary self writes him

long seductive letters, streaked in perfume, folded around
X-rated photos of her crotch and tits. My extraordinary self
was never subtle about anything, ever, but her pornographic

notes feel pedantic, and somewhat stale—an old dog's trick.
Of course, if he found them, he would like them. We all
know this. But my ordinary self is always first to the mailbox

and has learned not to open and read. Instead, she tears
the paper into kindling for the grill, to feed and stoke a fire
over which she'll cook the family a wholesome meal.

A Clean, Level Plane

Remember the lines in my extraordinary self's face?
The crease above her nose. Wires of gray electing
to stand from her head. And the veins rising like

tunneled land across her hands, or else spreading thin,
blue roots down the trunks of her legs. There's a toll
she paid. My ordinary self, however, budgets her energies.

There's no light at the end of the tunnel because
the tunnel doesn't exist. My ordinary self is a clean,
level plane. Her body is not parceled for worry

to burrow through. Each night, a regimen: immortelle oil
and cuticle cream. Always to bed at the same time.
She remains smooth as the least troubled sleep.

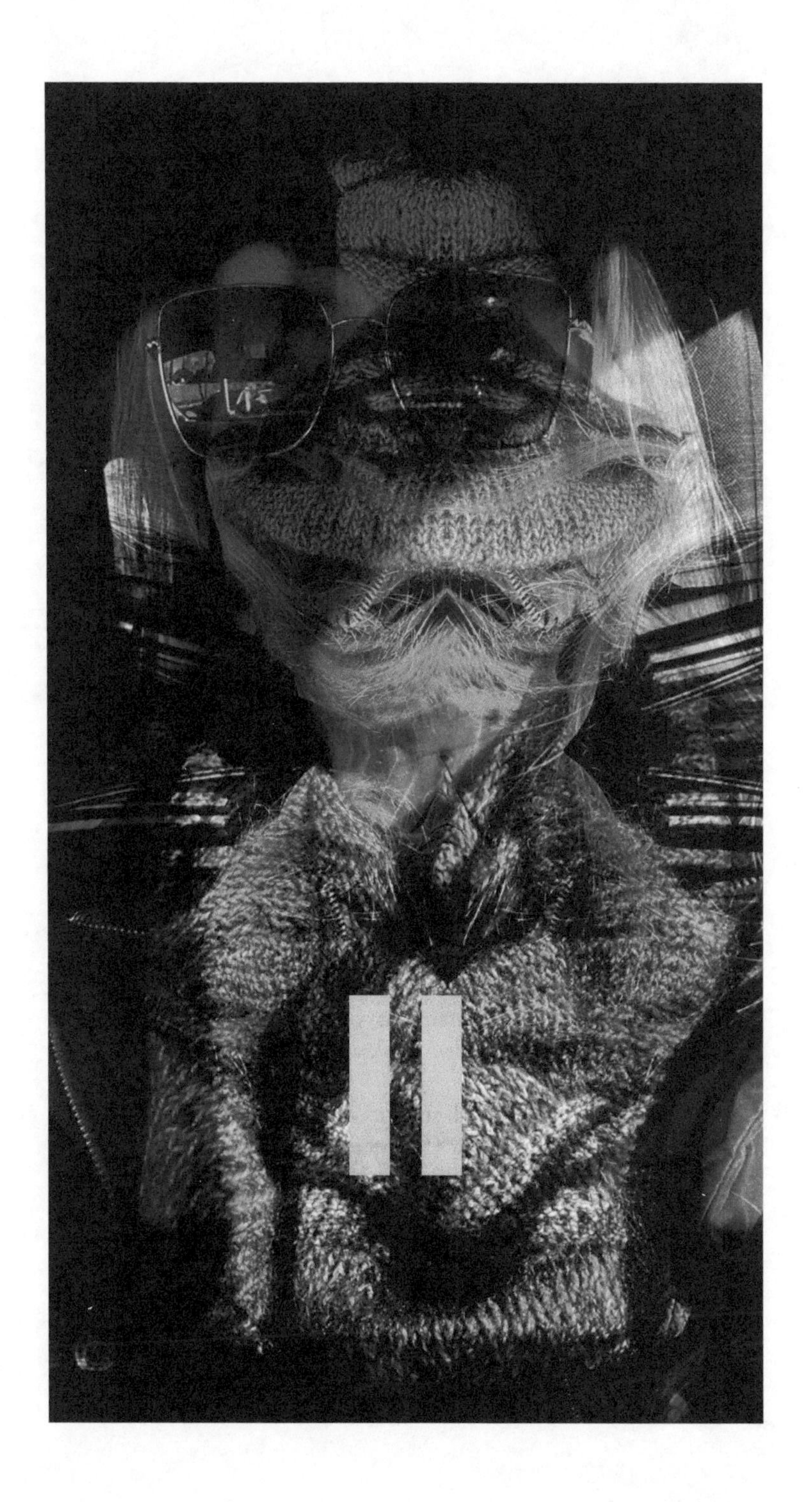
II

Her Terror is Palpable

When she can't sleep, my extraordinary self abandons
her bed for the car. She listens to rain hitting the roof,
watches it loop down the windshield and disappear

beneath the hood. Sometimes she takes a cup of tea
and stares as the liquid transforms to steam, smoke-like
wraiths rising to meet her chilled face. She's haunted

by ghosts, of course, has always endured their cliché, banal
arrival: always at night, always with a show of low crying,
rustling sheets, banging doors, and furtive, moving shadows.

Often, they follow her to the car. The Ghost of
My Extraordinary Self Past feels most at home in the back playing
with seatbelt buckles and making requests for radio stations,

but she's never happy with what's played. Eventually she'll settle
for an abandoned channel and its static song. The Ghost of
My Extraordinary Self Present prefers the front passenger side,

insists on adjusting the air vents, moves the seat back
and forth: reclined then upright. She never stays with one
position for long. It's the Ghost of my Extraordinary Self

Yet to Come who's least companionable. She manifests
in the trunk, and though my extraordinary self refuses
to walk around and release the door, we know somehow

this ghost is blindfolded, gagged, and trussed with rope.
Her terror is palpable. She thumps her head and moans.
But my extraordinary self turns up the static on the radio,

and wills the night to sheet the car with its wet noise.
Then morning comes, or the rain pauses, the ghosts
dissolve, and she sleeps in the brief, elliptical quiet.

A Necessary Lesson

Lest you think we're judging my extraordinary self
extremely and unfairly, know that she's kind of a shit:
Perpetually cranky with the kids because she can't have

more quiet, or more time, or simply more of her way;
distraught when odds are stacked against her and small requests
from the children—for a glass of water, a repeated direction,

or braided hair—stand like roadblocks in her path
to some imagined greatness. I mean, really, she's the worst.
Don't waste time over her spilt ambitions, opaque as milk—

they were too much for such a small glass. It's a lesson
she must learn. So turn your head and pretend you don't
hear when she says *I'm sorry*; or better yet, stare her down

as she avoids meeting your eyes over our boy's shoulder,
whom she hugs at the bus stop, trying to dam his tears
at her sleeve. *Please forgive me*, she whispers. Yet don't relent.

Her sorrow's sincere, but like hindsight, late. The boy,
your gaze, and time's critique: each should be as unrelenting,
as dagger-sharp and piercing, as cold as November's sleet.

That Worn Joke (It Cuts and Bleeds)

One summer week, the kids enrolled in camp,
my extraordinary self and I meet after morning drop-off.
Each time she orders the same: Small regular, black;

egg white omelet. *I am trying,* she says, *to be more disciplined. Less erratic*. In the coffee shop everyone likes her.
She's quiet, neat, and aloof. Friendly when she needs to be.

The baristas look her in the eyes. By midweek regulars
save her a corner table. *You have a great smile,* they tell her.
The feminists lied, she tells me. *They said we could do everything*

we wanted. Anything, I correct her. *And what's a girl like you reading feminists for, anyway?* She grins. That worn joke.
The man to her left sees white teeth flash and looks up.

What are you writing? he asks. *My life's work,* she answers.
We all look down. Between cross-outs and arrows, one word
loops over and over. Through the pages it cuts and bleeds.

Stop Her Before She Speaks

My ordinary self practices augury, reading the oils
topping her coffee like others dredge meaning
from tea leaves stuck to the cup's bottom.

Through the shifting steam she sees omens swirl forth,
as if conjured, glossy and black. But she's a cheap
Cassandra, her prophecies so banal no one cares

if they speak the truth or no. The children have learned
to tune her out: they nod acknowledgment, then
their eyes turn carnival-token cold. And my husband

stopped listening months ago. A bit of the magician himself,
he can foretell her visions, and stops her before she speaks.
Nothing makes her feel more like a sham than this:

hearing her thoughts from his mouth before she gives voice
to them. She's an oracle armed only with the most obvious
sight, a cold reader in a bathrobe. He sees her face

and exits quickly. He doesn't intend to be cruel,
but goddamn. Even her magic is ordinary. Her coffee
is just coffee, after all: it reveals nothing. It grows cold.

Patterns We've Sought

My extraordinary self lives her life guided by
our horoscope: love, health, ambition. *What value*
can our actions hold, she muses, *if they contradict*

the stars? My ordinary self has always laughed at this:
to believe in fate as shaped by patterns we've sought
in gas and flame. *We are blinded*, she scoffs, *when we turn*

our eyes to the sky. My extraordinary self admits she loves
that feeling most of all—opening the dark of her eyes
to sun, its white-out obliteration, the next few seconds

filled with the world's gradual dilation—but she finds
clarity, not obfuscation, in the night's black margins
surrounding white type, the stars' meter regular

as a sonnet. She insists: *Pay attention*: Lost light,
gained shadow. The honeysuckle's aphrodisiac scent.
The wind's deft touch, moving ribbons of cloud

to mark the wide, open page above our heads.
If we can't read the poems written there, she says,
we've lost something greater than our sight.

Beauty in Sameness

My ordinary self admits routine can be tiring.
Patterns in sleep, in meals, in tasks—the same day
repeating like a quilt, no matter how you fold it.

She knows the tedium of decent sleep: forgoing
a good book, TV deprivation. She knows
the drone of a better diet: the salad spinner's whir,

the Santoku's rhythm cleaving garlic. She knows
the blanched, bland flavor of the same path
run at the same early hour every day.

And yet, she says. The deer eating grass at dawn.
The water lit orange by sunrise and its salt-rim
taste. Pre-storm waves mouthing the shore

and wind bending beach grass. *Remember, there*
can be beauty in sameness, she says. *More than comfort,*
it gives us space for awe. She raises her arm toward

the waning moon—its less-than-brilliant cut, edges
softened by blue sky, and yet, miraculous:
its soft glow a worry stone cupped in her hand.

Beneath These Waves

It is a little bizarre to celebrate a birthday with one of us
in exile, but even my extraordinary self cannot stop
the roll of this tide. At least, that's what my ordinary self says

after she wakes—one hour past the alarm, a special indulgence—
and carries out her morning ritual: coffee, gratitude journal,
feed the dog, start some laundry. *Everything I want or need*

is right here, she tells the children when they present
their homemade cards. I groan and roll my eyes, which
she ignores as she begins to frost our cake. *Really, it's just*

another day, she says, but licks sugar from the knife.
Somewhere in the city, men are buying my extraordinary self
drinks. She's told them she's turned another year younger.

She is all buoyancy and jubilance and flashing teeth.
An entire bar sings, her newly devoted friends wishing her
the best, until last call rings. It's after three when she stumbles

into her room at the W, strips by the open windows, and lays
her naked body down on impossible-thread-count sheets.
In the pre-dawn dark, some of the city lights go out like candles

snuffed by a wish. She turns the noise machine on high, but
it sounds too much like the steady advance of encroaching ocean
tides: beneath their waves she loses her breath and cannot sleep.

We Must Be Ruthless

Although they may resemble something ancient and wise,
turkeys are not extraordinary creatures. Their lack of guise
and passion, however, fascinates my ordinary self to no end.

When the wild hen brings her young into our yard,
one ungainly bird at a time hopping the fence, she finds herself
staring, caught by the mother's onward march despite a chick

that remains just beyond the gate. To its mother's ears its distress
is unremarkable, like our late summer garden gone to weed,
and she proceeds to search for slugs among the grasses,

while the jake laments his place. Days later we will find
his abandoned shell on a neighbor's easement, neck broken,
missing eyes already eaten. And weeks after that we spy

the flock again, one chick short, but the mother's stride just
as long as before. My ordinary self's gaze narrows. She nods.
Don't you see, she says. *We must be ruthless to do this job.*

Let Others Create

My ordinary self watches the scout ant's frenetic search
along the picnic table and sees in its crazed diligence
our extraordinary self, trapped, in miniature. She feels

both pity and relief: to not be that. To avoid such busyness
means that someone else will have to be the scout
while she remains the worker. My ordinary self believes

in industry, doing the good and difficult work, but good
and difficult work is not singular. Millions of ordinary people
all over the world do good and difficult work daily.

Like worker ants marching in the pheromone line, they
are the infertile and wingless caste bred to build and sustain.
My ordinary self knows that to avoid the extraordinary means

minimizing risk, to deny the unknown. She is content
to let others create the trail, to follow their exceptional lead.
And yet: when the scout ant scurries near, she crushes it.

The Coin Lands Here

If I keep reaching out, is my extraordinary self really
in exile? Like early August mornings in the south,
our meetings feel deceptively cool. They lack intensity,

the atmosphere tense but like a rubber band stretched
until its fibers pull loose, but not to its snapping
point. We sit across from each other, opposing sides

on a penny, but usually with some peace proffered.
A hand on the table. An anecdote about the weather.
Waiting to be flipped, to see where we will land,

who will win this toss. To some extent we both
feel in upheaval. I resent my ordinary self's routines
as much as I need them: so many hospital corners

and lists of next actions. I miss my extraordinary self,
her chaos, her distraction, her enthusiasm for every new,
shiny thing. On one occasion, I tell her so. She stares at me,

her wordless anger like a white sun approaching its zenith
or a copper cent spun on glass. Her silent disdain rolls
to a stop. She opens her mouth. The coin lands here.

Between Past and Future

Maybe life has been easier because we exiled
my extraordinary self and her impossible expectations,
or maybe it was just vacation's freedom, its casual pace

held down by heat and humidity. She feels apprehensive
either way, my ordinary self, about the end of summer.
She sweats now, watching the calendar discard pages

like deciduous trees and the children clamor for back-
to-school shopping trips. There is one persistent hot pink
bloom on the boxy azalea in the yard. She resents its

audacity—holdover from spring, the old regime—
and wants to rip it out. Instead she waits, forcing herself
to look for its open, exotic face every time she exits

the house or returns home. Her shirt sticks to her back.
A thin film rides the lines of her temples. She's always
loathed azaleas. How long will it take for the blossom

to drop into the mulch? Autumn's congestion approaches,
but spring's mistakes wink from the garden corner. Between
past and future, she struggles like a fly adhered to paper.

To Escape This Trap

My ordinary self practices self-care. She gives herself
space to breathe—meditation in the morning, yoga
in the afternoons, and forgiveness if she misses a session.

She says my extraordinary self would have accomplished
more if she'd just learned how to focus on the breath,
a white light that washes us from the inside-out

if we pay close attention to it. *We always have the breath,*
my ordinary self says. My extraordinary self thinks this is
horseshit, spits the word vehemently to show disdain.

Yet her breath catches as she speaks, a tense gathering
in her breast just near the clavicle, all the tendons taut
and poised as dancers and ready to escape this trap, our body.

As if they could. *I know how to breathe,* she says. *There's no
white light.* And she's right, despite the way her lungs hold
the morning chill: Eventually, she exhales a cloud like smoke.

With Every Disappointment

Occasionally and always on the sly, my extraordinary self
visits the children. My eldest daughter, easily influenced,
gives her a key and humors her crazy fantasies about

taking a trip, flying to Italy, walking the bridges of Venice
before they become home to coral, another city besieged
by man and water. They are co-conspirators,

the globe of my daughter's open, hopeful face antipodal
to my extraordinary self's lost faith. My daughter imagines
she will somehow leave too, a tiny travel companion beside

her adventurer mother, until it becomes apparent that
my extraordinary self never intends to take her. *You always
do this*, my daughter sobs, *you make promises and then*

you break them. For once, my extraordinary self is satisfied.
This is a gift, she tells my daughter. *Be less like me. With every
disappointment, grow certain of what you won't become.*

I Make a Fractured Promise

Just when she thinks she's begun to make a difference
in our home, my ordinary self finds evidence
of my extraordinary self's surreptitious visits,

pockets of disorder and chaos appearing erratically
as if my extraordinary self were some malevolent faery
doing harm in incremental, nonsensical ways.

My husband shrugs and sighs and says something stoic
about habits and personality, then walks outside
to mow the lawn. The children don't find any of it

particularly upsetting, but remark in awe
when my ordinary self repairs or cleans the mess—
it's so nice in here, they enthuse. *We should keep it like this*

always. Sometimes my ordinary self wants to stick
her head in the oven—but that's only one of the places
she has yet to clean, and, after all, it's an expression.

Even my ordinary self has a sense of humor, however
macabre. But she has difficulty laughing about
my extraordinary self's attempts to thwart her efforts,

and my complicity. In the bathroom mirror, betrayal's
scar is plain, like a severe burn that distorts and melts
the face. It's so difficult to witness—I have to look away.

I whisper apologies toward the tiled floor, but her eyes
follow me. I splash some water, wipe down the sink.
I make a fractured promise. *I'll do better*, I say.

Her Blandness is Camouflage

My ordinary self remembers not to sweat the small
stuff at work. Memos about accountability
and company-wide expense cuts fall like raindrops

across her inbox; someone leaves signs in the breakroom,
above the microwave, another beside the copier.
Essentially, they say: *Clean Up Your Mess, Don't Break Shit.*

Customers fill her office doorway with bloated,
opaque demands, and always the imperative NOW
riding their lips. But my ordinary self has vowed

to focus on the mundane tasks, all to serve
her ordinary mission, and so she takes the specs
and writes the bids; keeps her meals at lunchtime cool

and splatter-free; refrains from copy jobs that make
the machine lumber toward its limit. She keeps her head
down, eyes low, except to smile when there's a need.

Even her sweaters match the paint, her shoes the carpet.
If she sits still at her desk, aside from her typing fingers,
her blandness is camouflage: she's the woman no one sees.

It is Difficult to Say the Word

I ask my ordinary self if she is happy. It is difficult
to say the word. Her own voice trembles
as she says it back to me like a question,

and her eyes focus on the trees beyond our driveway,
down the block, as if she expects someone to arrive soon.
To be fair, it's a trick question: Why does everyone feel

entitled to happiness, as if it were as common
or as necessary as oxygen? She says she feels content.
She knows the difference. I know the difference.

Together we look down the road, content
with each other's company, but curious about
who or what might come around the corner.

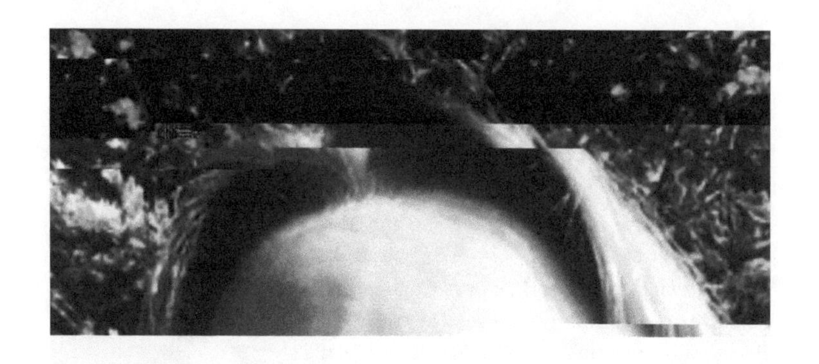

III

Eventually Bodies Tire

My extraordinary self is extraordinarily cunning,
and convinces my husband to make the trip to Italy
very real. *Pack light*, she tells him, *and leave the true*

baggage behind, and here she'd be giving my ordinary self
side-eye, if my extraordinary self was allowed in the house.
Because this meeting with him is rare and on the sly,

and time won't remain on pause while they rendezvous
in the car, she bites his ear lobe and rubs his crotch,
and soon they both forget about my ordinary self

and her fiduciary caution. If my ordinary self was here,
she'd remind him about the schedules not our own,
and placed in unromantic upheaval: the childcare

to be arranged, pet-sitters booked, employers told,
the mails put on hold, house-sitters engaged.
But she isn't around to nag or put this capricious plan

into a more staid perspective, so instead his head
is filled with gondolas and Sicilian beaches,
and my extraordinary self is smiling as she tongues

his neck and jaw. She thinks she's back, from exile
or retirement, and perhaps, in this moment, she is—
but seduction and travels end, eventually bodies tire

and everyone wants to sleep or eat a sandwich.
And there's our home, where my ordinary self remains
in gathering dust and unpaid bills, feeding on her anger.

More Fanatic than True Practitioner

Part of her undoing is my extraordinary self's greed,
her obsessive need to do it all. Like a martyr,
but certainly not selfless, her devotion to pet projects

borders on bodily: she will sacrifice herself to herself
like an ancient god just to make creation happen.
And, like true martyrdom, it ain't pretty.

Fewer entrails, perhaps, but still the stench of what
belongs inside being placed without. Degradation
on display. She thinks this path is true, the artist's way.

Of course, she couldn't be more wrong
and my ordinary self, while not well-versed
in acts of art or modes of creativity, knows a tire fire

when she sees one. She watches my extraordinary self's
desperate pilgrimage toward some holy land
she loosely understands; she is more fanatic

than true practitioner. My ordinary self may prefer
material trappings, but her attention to minutiae proves
more productive than any zealot's prayers or effusions.

A Feast for Some Other Being

When we were much younger, my extraordinary self
thought we might live a more extraordinary life overseas.
A work permit, a lump of credit, and ambition were all

we claimed at customs. But when we opened our suitcase
inside the cramped bedsit, a fist of stowaway moths
jettisoned from our clothes. All right—that's a stretch—

no swarm attacked my face, our faces, yet a single moth did
hitch a ride and when we unzipped the bag, it escaped.
It probably lived for one more day. My/our jaw fell open

as we stared at its gray wings struggling in the cooler,
post-flight air. Its equally gray light. In that moment,
our future felt full of holes: a feast for some other being.

Not our own. We stared at the insect, all three amazed,
our shock a solidarity. My extraordinary self, absent of context
or praise for the first time in years, felt utterly, terribly alone.

The First Real Darkness

Allow me this brief derailment from our story, please:
that first time we went overseas marked the first real
darkness we'd ever known. Absent from their usual

surroundings, my ordinary and extraordinary selves
had no idea what to do. London was a city that gave
no fucks about our charms, whatever we imagined them

to be. I was on my own for once—my ordinary
and extraordinary selves remained inside my rented room
while I left for work each day. I was a walking hull,

and they stayed curled under the borrowed goose-down
coverlet, to which we were allergic, listening
to the other tenants come and go, speaking of punk rock

shows or takeaway they'd ordered for delivery. We lived
off crisps and the rare Pret A Manger sandwich,
which is why, despite our poverty, we gained so much stone

those first few months. That, and the shifting seasons ate
the daylight. Starved for sun, we woke up early in the gray-
black dawn and, instead of running, stared at our sad,

pale reflections. And then I left for work to help my boss
drink himself deeper into his living death. It had all
the signposts of a Hallmark made-for-TV movie, really.

I was that hapless, ridiculous protagonist whose
turning point crested with date rape, the falling action
really no action at all, just more stasis—maybe

a melodramatic crying jag or two, but then the flight home,
heavy with defeat. I wore my limp and useless ordinary
and extraordinary selves like heavy stoles in the airport,

piggybacked on my shoulders. Customs: the usual nightmare.
We had little of interest to declare on our return. We slumped
our way back into the States, with nothing to show but some

clichéd trauma and the many virginal pages in our passport.
And then, like good telenovela heroines, we suffered
amnesia: we forgot our pain and its potential lessons.

My Heart, Not Hers (And Not Hers Either)

If not for Buffalo Wild Wings and their extra large beers,
my husband might have divorced my extraordinary self
right at the airport. A man traveling with the least wise

version of his wife needs a drink, or two, or three,
because she will test all of *his* versions. Perhaps this is where
we acknowledge this conceit is not unique, nay, not

extraordinary: we all house within our skin and brains
another self or two, whole persons devoted to one aspect
of twenty-first century life with particular, not entirely

healthy, focus. Because I fought to maintain my own
shit-show of personalities, I'm not sure which version
of my husband sat with that version of myself

at the airport bar, eating fried whatever. All I know is that
on the plane, afterward, separated from him by rows
and crammed between two Baby-Boomers who didn't

want to share their vacant center seat, my heart burned:
part indigestion, sure, but with a moment of clarity.
It was *my* heart, not *hers*, and not *hers* either.

In the scratched chairback TV screen I saw my reflection,
its schism more raw and obvious than ever. *Why had I
brought us here?* Outside, the black tarmac winked its lights

as the jet roared. Seat belt signs sang their warnings.
Trailing tissue with her shoe, my extraordinary self
returned crying from the bathroom. The stewards tried

to soothe her with another drink, a different seat.
Several rows behind, my husband settled with relief, grateful
for this brief respite from all of me. And then we took off.

Neither Here nor There

In Venice my extraordinary self can't get out of her own way,
or anyone else's, for that matter. She is always walking
against the flow of foot traffic or standing amazed at some

fresco while bodies logjam behind her. Perpetually taking
too much space, misreading social cues, miscounting
euros, paying far too much for Moreno glass:

She is extraordinarily bad at being extraordinary
in such a setting. The green waters of the lagoon,
the singing gondoliers, the basilica and bells of San Marco,

even the Iraqi bartender in the Irish pub: all are spectacular
in their ambivalence. Here, she is just another tourist:
at best a quieter, more polite American, but mostly

a vague annoyance, a vulgar economic necessity,
but a mark so easy most pickpockets don't even bother.
You know, by now, how much that kills her. She is,

in everyone's eyes, neither here nor there. So much so
that when she returns to the airport the automated
doors hold fast: Her presence fails to register.

Useless Masks

What we don't realize at first is that my ordinary self
has accompanied us, like a stowaway moth but more ominous,
less pretty. First, let's say it: My poor husband. Three wives.

Next, let's acknowledge how lucky she is, my ordinary self,
having become thin and malleable as a scarf, folding like silk
into our carry on, since the Italians lost my extraordinary self's

luggage in Rome. She could have been in her own dark exile
for days, motion sick from the constant circle and drop
of conveyor belts and jet fuel's overly-present perfume.

But she's here, albeit in secret, kind of, like an elf or fairy
who appears at night to pick underwear off the floor.
She's not entirely sure why she came—she dislikes

change, standing in lines, sleeping in strange beds,
the lack of WiFi. She misses the children. But she likes
the Italians, with their clarity of voice and vision:

what their mouths don't shape they say with their hands
and arms. So different from the way we are, every conversation
a static of false starts, *our* arms strapped across our chests

like life vests, hands cupped at our lips in useless masks.
This weird plane, my fucked-up collection of selves, loses
pressure by the second, moves faster toward the ground.

We Can't Have Everything

For a few days we manage to make it work. It's easy
to distract my extraordinary self with food and drink
and art while she pretends to be better than the trappings

of tourism. We leave my ordinary self at the hotel,
a renovated glass factory, and she wanders its maze
of hallways, tapping on random doors, pretending

to be housekeeping. At one point she busses
the hotel's rooftop bar, shooing away scavenging pigeons,
collecting empty glasses. Some Americans leave a tip.

She's always been good at this, appearing to belong,
nodding her head and saying *Si* in response to most
directives. And then one night, a fog rolls in and no one

can come or go, and she's forced to watch my husband
and my extraordinary self from afar. She notes the bottles
of wine, the elegant pasta course, the swordfish

and swiss chard. How in love with her he seems:
how free from anxiety's register the low and high notes
of their conversation. *Why can't I have that?* she wonders,

then remembers that she was never supposed to be in Venice.
Such a scene for my ordinary self was never a possibility.
Eventually she stops this torture and shuts her eyes

to everything but the task at hand: turn-down service.
She smooths the sheets, scatters rose petals, fills the wine
bucket with ice. But she steals my extraordinary self's

bedside mint. Rolling it between her teeth like a bead,
she grimaces at her reflection in the mirror. *You can't
have everything.* Then she removes the hard candy

from her mouth and places it beneath my extraordinary self's
side of the mattress, like the proverbial pea. *Sleep on that,*
she thinks, melting back into shadow. *Fuck you and your dreams.*

To Be Present and Enjoy

My extraordinary self discovers my ordinary self
hiding inside an armoire and shit hits the fan. *Why can't I*
ever escape you, she groans, then cries, throwing her body

across the bed and weeping into a pillow. Her wails blend
with those of the alley cats below our window. I've sent
my husband to the hotel bar. As much as couples share,

there's no need for him to see this drama, my ridiculous
soap opera lurching toward yet another of a million
turning points. I try to deescalate my ordinary self's panic,

my extraordinary self's hysteria, with hazelnuts and wine.
Chew these, drink this, and let's lay some ground rules,
I insist. My extraordinary self agrees to the plan, but then

brings out a bottle of ouzo gifted by some Greek fellow
in Milan. *It tastes bitter*, my ordinary self frowns.
She refuses to leave the shadows of the armoire.

She's taken all the garments and rehung them, light
to dark. On this side of the room, my extraordinary self
pours another round and complains about the temperature,

then rhapsodizes about where we'll travel next.
But the children, but our home, but our job, my ordinary self
objects. My extraordinary self rolls her eyes and shuts

the armoire doors, my ordinary self still tucked inside.
I remain at the window, watching the other guests
congregate in the hotel garden. *How reasonably*

they all behave, I murmur, *allowing themselves to be present,*
to enjoy, to have all this: the robust scent of thyme trampled
underfoot; stars scattered like aniseed across silent black sky.

Despite My Schisms and Rifts

My husband and I escape my other selves at some point
during our European trip and spend an afternoon
beside a Spanish fortress in a medieval Sicilian city.

The mountain drops cumulus into the valley below
and we watch the mist stretch its gray screen before our eyes
and then remove it to reveal the brilliant terra cotta roofs

of the seaside town, like hotel staff closing doors to hide
their ritual housekeeping, something private and precious
and sacred. This stolen time, our asses growing pitted

from the eroded rock, our mouths softening under
the influence of gift-shop wine sipped from plastic cups,
is glorious. We haven't been this alone for years.

Look, we're inside a cloud, we say out loud, overheard
only by a dead snail and German tourists making out
on a cliff at some short remove. Neither respond nor seem

to mind our banality, our obviousness, and so we indulge
in the pleasure of an unpurposed hour. We joke,
we philosophize. I forget my ordinary and extraordinary

selves in that moment. They are probably waiting
like anxious dogs on the hotel balcony, careening
their necks and shifting every time they hear our laughter.

Absent of their embattled nonsense, divinely and wholly
free and with the man who loves me, despite my schisms
and rifts, I feel kinship with the lizards that dart, sudden

and unprovoked from scrub brush. They hesitate for seconds,
swivel their manic, ecstatic heads before the enormous panorama
and then leap, fast and hard, into the cottony unknown.

They Will Not Be Moved

As with most hangovers, I pay a price for my time away
from my divided selves. The extraordinary one sulks
spectacularly, really settling into a non-silence that bangs

the doors and shutters as if she were wind repeating
a guttural syllable. She refuses to sleep, instead hanging out
in the hotel lobby with off-duty staff she coaxes into having

one more drink, sharing one more story, before they go home
in the gathering storm. Her conscious laughter is a gale
combing the mountainside, loosening the tethers and bolts

in my mind, threatening to upend anything not tied down.
My ordinary self makes the bed while we're still in it,
talks a little too loudly about the baby lizard crawling

across the ceiling, insists on dragging us down to breakfast
even though we're all too tired to eat. Her courtesy
has an edge to it, a shrill quality like air moving fast

down a tin chimney flue. My extraordinary and ordinary
selves want my attention equally. They also hate me.
It's impermanent, this hatred: one more cold front

moving across the valley. Yet it's but a distraction from
their more vicious resentment of one another: *That* anger
is not changeable wind, but bedrock. It will not be moved.

Doubt and Awe

If poetry is the stuff of questions, my extraordinary self asks,
why do so many poems end with profound conclusions?
Where is doubt? Where is awe? She's drunk again, having

found an audience of traveling American writers—who
like wine and, for some reason, listening to this idiot talk.
My ordinary self, one table over, folds and refolds

a cloth napkin, pressing its corners into exactness.
Maybe we aren't reading them closely enough, she suggests.
Maybe we aren't reading them correctly. My extraordinary self

winks at the bespectacled men drinking at the table
and refills their glasses to the brims. *That*, she says,
is what the patriarchy would have you believe. Faulty readers.

My ordinary self frowns and leans forward, elbows
on her knees, jaw in her hands, eyes pitched toward the cliff
outside the window. *Questions in poems don't matter anyway*,

she says. *We have more than enough doubt and awe*
right here. And just like that, the tenor of the night
suddenly shifts, like fog descending, or a rock song

unplugged, its amplification and bass lines emasculated.
The gentlemen clear their throats and mutter in chorus,
something about rising early to write. My extraordinary

and ordinary selves are left sitting among half-empty
wine glasses scattered like question marks. *You gals*
really know how to clear a room, I say, and they nod.

We sit like that in silence for an hour before going
to bed, turning over the same question in our heads
again and again, but no closer to any answer.

An Absurd Lament

My ordinary self does what other ordinary persons do
abroad: take photos and buy things. Here, she finds
her people—whole crowds pointing cameras and sifting

Euros through their fingers like beads of Murano glass.
Because she is my ordinary self, even impulsive getaways
feature list after list: family who need souvenirs;

foods to try; duomos and basilicas and gothic arches
to stand under, open-mouthed. *Check, check, check.*
But the green waters of Venice, the boutique shops

off San Marco plaza—none of it translates well to film,
or looks as authentic under the hotel lamp's glare.
By the time we arrive in Sicily, she's begun to understand

why most ordinary people stay home. There are only
so many Italian cat t-shirts one can buy; customs
will allow only so many anchovy-wrapped almonds

past their gates. She won't admit it to any of us,
but she misses her ordinary diet and her ordinary
views. We can tell by the way she picks at her pastry

in the morning, how when we visit the Temple of Venus
she's more impressed by stray dogs and lisping toddlers
than the centuries-old stonework beneath her feet.

She sees the white caps cresting the Mediterranean
and—true story—she misses the Atlantic. By the week's
end, we can read her only as pathetic, myopic

in her vision's scope. She regrets her attempt to escape,
to be anything other than unremarkable and content.
She spends those last nights folding and refolding

clothes into the suitcase, next to the trinkets she bought.
She rehearses leaving as if spontaneity were a specter
to guard against, her humming an absurd lament.

A Moment That Shouldn't Exist

One afternoon my foolhardy extraordinary self becomes
lost on cobblestone streets, unsure where to turn and
unable to speak a syllable of Italian. *This is where*

impulsiveness leads us, she hears my ordinary self say
from the dark alleyways of her head. The narrow
medieval roads feel close but not cloistering; she can see

the sky and knows that should she find the perimeter,
the city's edge before the land topples into prayer,
she'll find her way back to the hotel and its curated views.

For now the worn faces of cherubs and foreign street signs
hang over her like a mantilla she's chosen to wear,
deference to a more extraordinary power. This is

markedly different from when she traveled to Los Angeles,
another city in which the language escaped her—
its syntax so singular, its day-lit streets a sinuous dialect

that shifted into something amorphous and messy with night.
No one wanders into Skid Row, and yet she did, my
extraordinarily stupid self. Few people aspire to be

a tourist attraction, especially those living in tents
on concrete city streets. That surface proved the most
difficult terrain she's ever walked, her gaze held low,

obvious and shamed. When the film crew tethered
to the flatbed truck sped by, she saw herself
through their lens—an absurd aberration in the landscape,

a moment that shouldn't exist. The memory ghosts her now;
every Italian she passes looks through her; and when she reaches
a parapet it appears: the urge to leap, a flame above her head.

Something That Must Remove

Sleep escapes my extraordinary self most nights.
At first she attempts to blame jet lag, time difference,
the hotel's unforgiving bed and rough sheets,

but by day six she's forced to admit—once again—
that she's the problem. Dropped inside new contexts
like Sicilian countryside has only proved

her inability to change, to be anything other
than what she was or is. She still sneezes
around Italian cats. She still eats and drinks too much

when offered cassatella and Italian brandy.
She thought she'd appear softer, less desperate
against the backdrop of dust-road switchbacks

and medieval cobblestone, but Italy has her panting
like the dog that howls past midnight most nights
when she tries to sleep but instead just aches

and aches. My extraordinary self has always known
but now, watching hours drop off the neon travel clock,
realizes—she cannot change this context, time,

or how her gross ambition becomes more evident
with each new day, like lines around her mouth and eyes.
She is essentially problematic, something that must

remove. She shifts and tries again to close her mind
to thought. On the bedside table, fruit flies swirl
and multiply inside an abandoned glass of wine.

Knowing Failure

When my ordinary self returns from Italy she sees
the effect of her absence: Dirt and disorder writ large.
Ordinary selves aren't allowed vacations, impromptu

passions, or rash decisions that result in debt and dust
and a fine coat of dog hair over it all. The children
have missed her, but resent being told to go to bed.

The house sitter graffitied the furniture with strange,
archaic symbols by etching stark lines in the grime
that covers every surface. It all points to a cleansing,

a necessary purging—even our email account is flooded
with memos from work, urgent questions from colleagues.
My extraordinary self doesn't even reenter the house—

instead, knowing the failure of her experiment, she remains
in exile, quieter and contrite. She drags her luggage back
across town to the motel, then spends the first evening

of her return pacing the shore of the river, a pale
but voiceless apparition. She pauses only to look at the moon.
Her eyes and mouth mirror its silent, singular O.

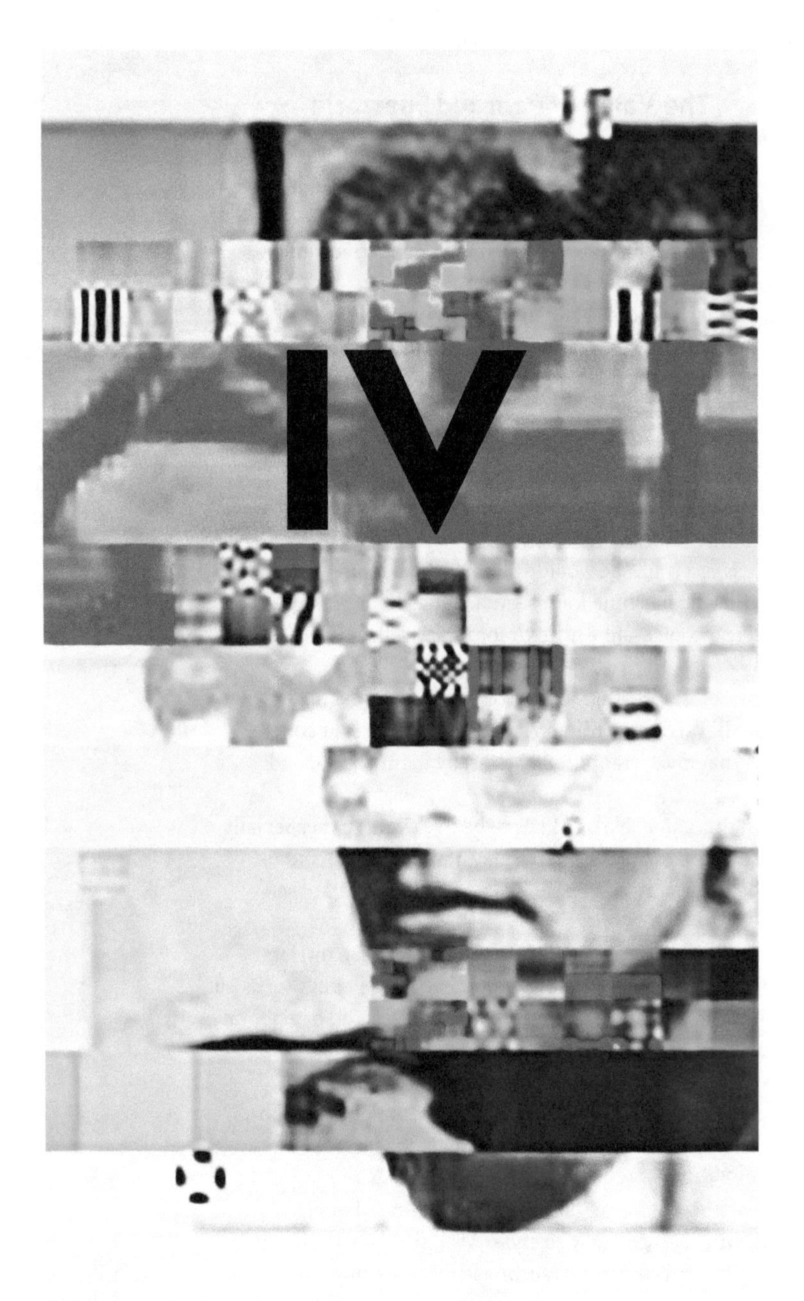
IV

The Value of Pain and Spectacle

For the first time, my ordinary self considers murder.
This is not an ordinary thing to do but she sees
few other options when faced with my extraordinary self's

repeat invasions, her deliberate transgressions.
After all, she reasons as she makes the children's lunches,
the best stories teach us: Never leave your enemies

alive. She smears the jam across the bread, cuts
the crusts, our daughter's sandwich a perfect square.
Poison won't work, she thinks. It's too messy,

leaves a trail, she wouldn't know which to use,
and who has time for research? It has to look
like a choice—like my extraordinary self, swayed

by defeat, breathless with sorrow, wanted to end
it all. What my ordinary self doesn't realize, of course,
is that my extraordinary self is, by nature, far ahead

in this game. No one likes to be irrelevant, but especially
someone shaped from the clay of possibility. Inside
her squatter's den by the river, my extraordinary self

has been cataloguing lists of possible ends: exorcism,
immolation, keelhauling, gibbeting, scaphism. It turns out
the more obscure the term, the more elevated or elaborate

its diction, the more brutal the means of death.
My extraordinary self has time for research. She knows,
too, the value of pain and spectacle, the lessons

both can serve, and if she does anything, damnit,
it will be to go out with style. Also, she'll need some help.
So my ordinary self is surprised one morning when,

after putting the children on the bus and waving
goodbye, she turns to find my extraordinary self
sitting on the stoop, a length of pale rope in her hand.

This is What We Chose

Faced with the reality of what she's being asked to do—
and yes, here you may laugh at my use of the word 'reality'—
my ordinary self swivels on the fine point of her loathing

and begins to wonder if there isn't another way. She says this
aloud as she and my extraordinary self disentangle
an abandoned dory from the patch of woods behind

my neighbor's house. *Of course there are other ways,*
my extraordinary self counters, *but this is what we chose.*
They work the boat free from the mud and vines,

push it along the grass down to the creek. The sunshine
is as flat as matte paint, the sky an ambivalent hue.
Down by the docks, the skiff lands with a splash, then rocks

back and forth, knocking against the piling. *It doesn't*
look like it will stay afloat, my ordinary self says,
watching water lip the scow's sides and turn the dusty

earth to mud. *That's not a bad thing, is it,* asks
my extraordinary self, although she directs the question
to the prow, its head split slightly, like a mouth

about to speak. *We'll move it to the reeds.*
Bamboo will support the boat. Raccoons and insects
and water snakes will do the rest. My ordinary self

shudders. *Even in death,* she grouses, *you have to be*
so extreme, so unnecessarily over-the-top.
Shut up, says the other one. And she jumps

into the dory's belly, lays her head against the stern.
Or would you prefer my possible return? My ordinary self
climbs into the boat and ties the binds in answer.

She paints milk and honey across her sister's hands,
face, limbs and feet. Then she empties the rest of the jar
into my extraordinary self's mouth, who drinks.

No Satisfactory Answer

For days my extraordinary self watches clouds at dawn
move across the sky. She waits to die, to be changed
into something better than this, like all of her attempts

over the years to make her extraordinary qualities manifest,
like a prophecy or an almanac's prediction come to pass.
Where are the bees? The aphids? She tries to catalog

all the insects she knows, worms and beetles interested
in a body's ruin. She faults, to some extent, the cat—
who arrived two days ago and licked most of the milk

and honey from her face, then moved methodically
to the rest of her skin—and now that she is clean as a kitten,
and albeit a little sick from the scow's constant bobbing

in the shallows, she concludes she feels fine. Even the cold
weather cannot burrow its way inside—because the cat,
like a totem, sits on her chest and purrs its comfort song.

This is not death, she thinks. Then at night the raccoons
and opossums arrive, but instead of chewing her skin
they gnaw free the ropes around her hands and feet,

sticky and sour with residue. And once they've left,
the water snakes curl beneath her arms, her flesh
a warm, comforting den in the absence of sun. And so,

within days, she concludes this experiment's done.
She's failed yet again. The worst part is walking past
my ordinary self making breakfast at the kitchen window.

My extraordinary self shuffles by, eyes down, trailing rope,
her savior cat pouncing behind. My ordinary self takes a bite
of toast and jam, watches my extraordinary self disappear

around the corner. *Well,* she thinks. *We must leave far less
to chance*. The gray morning's silence provides no satisfactory
answer, just the sound of her jaw as it pops and clicks.

A Greater, Deeper Need

My extraordinary self writes a list of possible ends,
hands them to my ordinary self for her perusal.
What next, she says. The pragmatic one takes her pen

and either checks or scratches out what meets or doesn't
with approval. *What I liked about the boats*, she thinks
aloud to her mirror image, *is that I didn't have to contend*

with the body. The waters of the creek were meant
to wash everything out to the bay. My extraordinary self
nods and looks away, beyond the sliding glass doors

to where Savior Cat stares at her from the deck.
My ordinary self follows her gaze. *And now,*
not only do we still have you, we have a pet.

They turn their eyes back to the list, heads close
and bowed together, and one would think they loved
each other, that like siblings or best friends

this companionship spoke of greater, deeper need
than their present task: deciding how best to eliminate
the one. Perhaps they do. Perhaps it does. And yet.

Authors of Their Own Sad Ends

Failing at death when you've already failed at life
is the ultimate kick in the nuts, isn't it?
asks my extraordinary self of my ordinary self.

They build a scaffold in the garage, attempt to fortify
against a body's swinging weight. *Think: Emma Bovary,*
her gruesome cartoon. Trying to sell what was left—

withered breasts, her desperate, janky eyes. But
thwarted by the gauche projectile vomit, black as crude.
My ordinary self has no reply, hands her a drill

and bolts. *Or*, my extraordinary self chatters on,
what about The Breakfast Club? Brian's shitty
elephant lamp, his impossible revolver. My ordinary self

nods, climbs the ladder into the attic space, waves
to signal she's ready for the reinforcing two-by-eight.
My extraordinary self passes it through, watches dust

and droppings fall between the beams. *But then again*,
she offers by way of killing silence, *they were fictional.*
My ordinary self peers down, clears her throat.

Remember seventh grade, social studies, the assassins
of the Archduke Ferdinand? My extraordinary self grimaces
as she raises the sister beam into place. *Expired cyanide.*

An empty riverbed. So many plot turns and yet
they were never authors of their own sad ends.
My extraordinary self laughs, a strangled bark.

That's not reassuring, she says. My ordinary self agrees:
We've been deceived. Fate is just another word
for accident. She tests the rafters. They sag with fatigue.

A Pendulum's Swing

So she swings from the rafters—recycles the rope
from the boats and ties a noose around her neck,
finds a bar stool to stand on and then kick away,

laces the other end around a beam and its brace,
pulls to check resiliency, whether the wood will hold
her weight. Everything appears as it should.

My ordinary self remains removed, apart,
sequestered inside the house, attending to chores.
She feigned a kind of nonchalance when saying

her final goodbye, a second time, the gesture
absurd as snow in June. It's November now,
and the season's creep has hastened to a crawl,

frost eating at the window panes, the creak
and pop of glass and wood expanding every time
she raises the heat. She turns up the radio, too,

tries to drown out her imagination, the sonic ghost
between her ears: a different kind of creaking,
a pendulum's swing, our extraordinary self dangling

above the garage floor concrete, her shadow
an impermanent stain no one will have to clean.
My ordinary self tries to stop her mind,

but it keeps arcing toward the garage. *We're better*
this way, she says to no one, or perhaps
to Savior Cat, who figure-eights around her feet.

A New Language

My extraordinary self appears at the back door, rope looped
like a scarf around her neck. *It didn't work,* she says.
Savior Cat, oblivious to her flat notes of humiliation and grief,

meows loudly. Its cat voice says: *rejoice!* My ordinary self
responds by picking up the feline, feeding it in the kitchen
with a can of tuna. *What happened this time?* she asks,

her fingers busy rubbing out grease spots on the stove.
The stool fell, the other says, *and my weight dropped fast.*
I should have felt nothing; witnesses would have heard a snap.

Yet no one but the mice were there, and they didn't seem
alarmed. I swung for hours: less air, a tightness about the throat,
but death did not approach. Huh, my ordinary self says.

I grew bored. Like, really bored; my view limited to what
I could see of my swaying feet and the sawdust and mouse
excrement on the floor. I must have begun to hallucinate,

because those droppings and wood dust started to shift.
Letters. A new language emerged. I saw the shape of my life.
I feel like I should write it down before I forget. My ordinary self

sighs and turns. *Only with you would failed suicide lead*
to delusions of grandeur. My extraordinary self counters,
Hey, I'm not done, and removes the rope from her shoulders.

One of these will work. Sure, says my ordinary self. *But even*
when we plot your death, look how ambition writes the script.
The kitchen clock ticks. Savior Cat paws its empty dish.

An Uneasy Ceasefire

Since she's engaged in the business of extermination,
my ordinary self decides to wage war against the insects
in the basement. Her one-time allies, they have multiplied

until she cannot walk through the laundry room without
crickets ticking against her ankles while others sing, a constant
chorus in a windowless chamber. Of late it grates against

her ears, chafes like the sound of my extraordinary self's voice
asking yet another question about death. My ordinary self
runs highways of sticky tape along the floor, creates water traps

in the corners. She boards up holes in the storage closet,
seals the gaps with expanding foam. But my husband
and children continue to leave the egress doors open at night,

and the windows of the cellar are old, the seams easy
to chew through. My ordinary self replaces the traps,
lays new bowls of water and glue, but still the insects

multiply. Unwilling to use pesticide, she wonders if this
is the conclusion to most conflicts, an uneasy ceasefire:
one side a field of torn and abandoned limbs, a population

diminished but not destroyed, and the other side grown
frustrated and bored, its taste for vengeance or domination
lost, who more or less shuts a door, shrugs, and walks away.

Destroyed, Not Reused

Let's put you and your cat in a bag and throw you in the river,
says my ordinary self. When my extraordinary self looks up,
her face contorted like crumpled paper, my ordinary self sighs

and rolls her eyes. *That's a joke,* she says. *You know I wouldn't*
do that to a kitten. She bends to stroke Savior Cat's back.
That's been happening a lot, hasn't it, says my extraordinary self.

Your exasperation. My loss of humor. She shuffles through
their research notes. *It's just,* begins my ordinary self. *I thought*
you'd be gone by now. I thought the drama would be over,

our life turned to rights. Instead, we talk more than we ever have
before. I see you daily. I wanted less than this, to be honest,
or maybe more, in a sense: a pervasive, overwhelming calm. Not

your ramshackle calamity. My extraordinary self lifts a sheet
of typescript and squints. *We could try immurement,* she suggests.
Hell no, says the other. *I want you out, not between these walls*

for all eternity. My extraordinary self balls the page and tosses it,
a sure shot, into the recycling can. She stares at the bin's
cobalt blue. *Well, if I can't be destroyed,* she muses, *perhaps*

I can be reused. My ordinary self laughs. *You're pretty thick.*
Or stubborn. I can't decide which. Either way, please listen
when I say: You need to be gone. Not made new, reincarnated,

reinvented. Just obliterated. It's the only way. My extraordinary
self whimpers. *But I can't do this.* The other grimaces.
How were you ever the special one? You're so boring.

Kill or Be Killed

This can't be fun for you, my extraordinary self says
to my ordinary self. *I don't imagine it is.* Together,
they drag all the paraphernalia from their failures,

my extraordinary self's impossible execution:
skeins of rope; wood from scaffolding; fist-sized
stones; a sleeping black mamba coiled in a basket;

the pistol my father brought back from Vietnam,
a bottle of Drain-O; and the portable generator,
a mask taped to the exhaust. For kitsch, a crown

of thorns. They pile it all at the property's far end.
My ordinary self moves to light a match. *Wait,*
my extraordinary self says. *You should probably*

keep the generator. Just burn the mask. While they
remove the machine from under all the other detritus,
the wicker basket falls and the mamba slithers away.

My extraordinary self shrugs. *It will kill or be killed,*
she says. Then she climbs atop the pyre. She dabs
gasoline on her neck and wrists and behind her ears;

my ordinary self splatters it like paint across the wood
and lights a new match. Flame catches and grows fat.
The mamba slithers back toward the heat, and above

the burning mess my extraordinary self sits, waiting
for the smoke and fire to do what they do best.
My ordinary self watches without words. Her hands

bend and twist the garden hose. Our other self stares
straight ahead, jaw set, surrounded by the fumes
from materials not intended for open flame. Smoke

blacks the air of the yard and coats the trees. It takes
hours for it all to dwindle down to the stones, which
remain, along with my seething extraordinary self,

covered in char and soot. My ordinary self has fallen
asleep in an Adirondack chair, the mamba curled
around her feet. My extraordinary self wakes her

with a small touch to the shoulder. *Well, you're no
phoenix, that's for sure,* she says with a yawn.
They wet and spread the ashes across the lawn.

Then Where Would We Be?

So an exorcism, says my extraordinary self. *We need*
a priest? My ordinary self is sorting through the kitchen
storage cabinet, a small closet filled with mismatched

plastic covered in dirt and animal hair, the result
of children playing freely with its contents. *Or a shrink*,
she answers. *I think our situation calls for something*

heavier than prayer and dime-store vials of Holy Water.
My extraordinary self reaches out for the broken
and warped pieces, deposits them in the recycling bin.

They're dollar-stores now, old timer, she says. *And maybe*
a practitioner of made-up faith is what we need, all things
considered. Pausing in her snap-lock, press-seal matching,

my ordinary self shoos Savior Cat out of the way. *If we're*
truly figments of imagination, she says, *why does my back hurt*
from sitting on this floor? If you're fictional, how'd you manage

to fuck things up so well? And how do we have fourteen lids
and nine containers? My extraordinary self raises her eyes,
sees stars from the kitchen's bright fluorescent lighting.

Your back hurts because you're old, she says. *And maybe*
most people are nothing but collections of small narratives,
mismatched anecdotes and tales of trial and tribulation.

Appendices of cliché and rite-of-passage stories. My ordinary
self moves a pile of acceptable pairs to the sink for washing.
Christ, she says. *Maybe we just want stronger meds*.

She watches dog and cat fur swirl around the drain.
But we might lose you, too, says my extraordinary self.
And then where would we be? Good question,

I answer from my seat at the kitchen table.
My selves startle in response, and then stare
at each other. They'd forgotten. I was in the room.

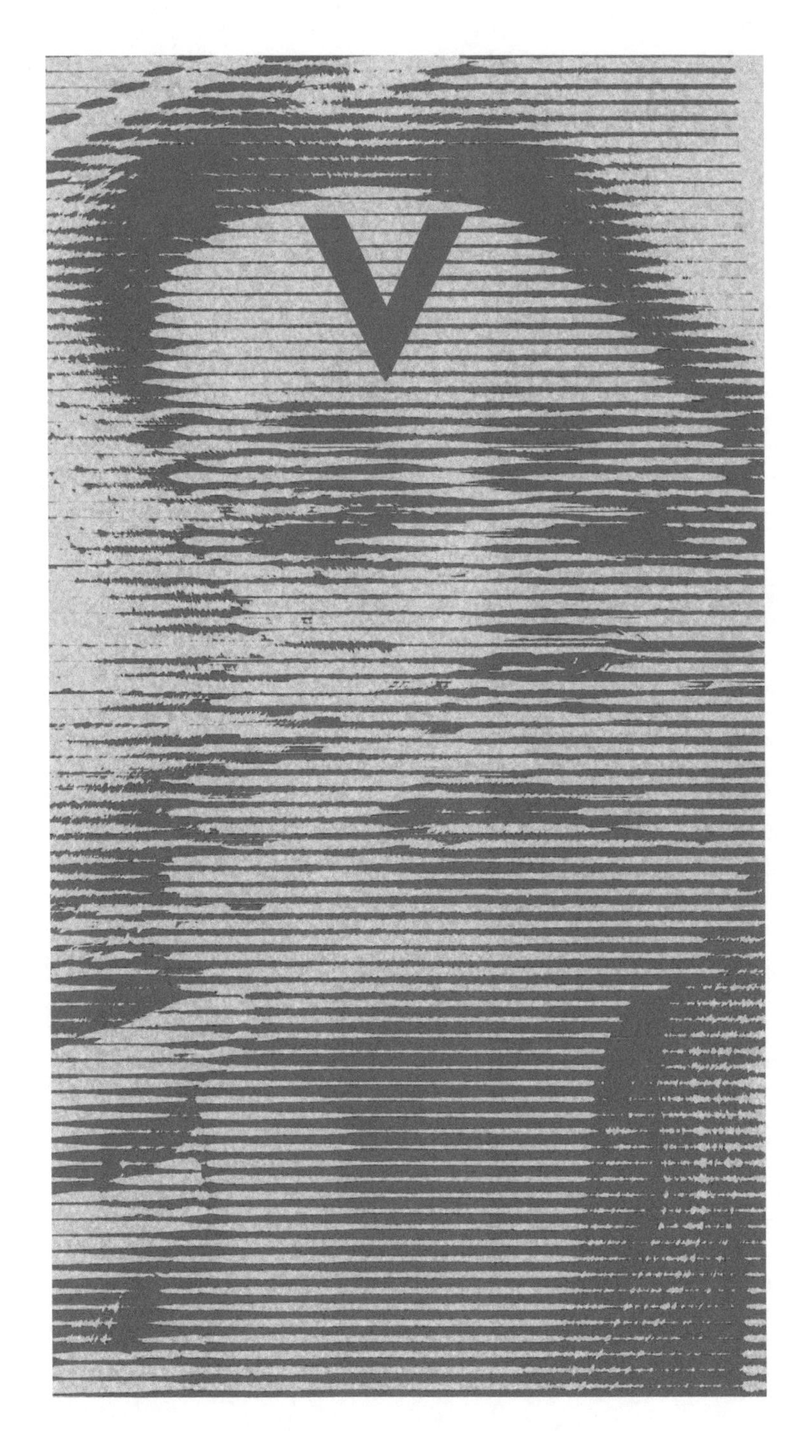
V

Move It or Lose It

Carpetbag in hand, my inevitable self arrives at the house
just when we think we've reached our limits. At least
she knocked. For weeks my poor family's been weaving

around my extraordinary and ordinary selves, who've taken
to standing still in the oddest, most inconvenient places.
My ordinary self likes doorways, as if they're portals

to another life, or as if she's sure the house will crash down
on all our heads at any moment. My extraordinary self
prefers the center of rooms, where like an ornate pillar

in an ill-conceived theatre, she obstructs our view
of the TV's nightly news or our path from kitchen
to dining room. Every exit, every leaving in this house

has become a negotiation. (And lord, the weeping!)
Anyway, my inevitable self arrives and sees it all—
my children orbiting their divided mother, the dog

chewing worry holes into his memory-foam bed,
my husband asleep in the afternoon—because how else
does one avoid the tears and endless monologues

of so many wives? My inevitable self walks in, calls
the children, gives them hard candy, sends them outside
to play. She's brought the dog a bone. Then she thwacks

my extraordinary self across the calves with her assistive cane.
Move it or lose it, honey, she says, *and wipe your nose.*
My extraordinary self nods slowly and drifts to the edge

of the room, rests an arm on the too-high bookshelf.
She looks out of joint and in pain, but at least she's not
in the way. For a few minutes, nothing but the sound

of a lozenge rolling between teeth. My inevitable self nods
and hands me her bag. Her cataract eyes survey the mess,
take in more than I would wish. My ordinary self coughs,

curious and alarmed, from her spot at the basement ingress,
where she slumps against the doorjamb. *Find me a chair,
will you?* says my inevitable self. *We have a lot to do.*

The Gang's All Here!

My inevitable self has lost most of her teeth. *A sign of wealth,*
she chuckles, and gums her food with relish. *That's dreams,*
mutters my ordinary self from her post by the bathroom door.

My inevitable self grunts, *eh?,* oatmeal thick in her mouth.
If you dream of losing your teeth . . . but my ordinary self's voice
drops away like cereal clumped at the old woman's lips.

My extraordinary self, her own face cradling a wordless O,
her eyes lit white and large, can't or won't speak. Savior Cat spies
the falling cereal and places its paws on my older self's thigh,

teeth and tongue raking her polyester slacks for scraps. *Well
look at us,* my inevitable self cries, thumping the table
and grinning. *The gang's all here!* None of us can meet her eyes.

Her Shape Flickers and Shifts

My inevitable self is a bag of old tricks. And yet, she's not easy
to imagine—her shape flickers and shifts. One moment,
she's a summation of stress-eating multiplied over years,

her skin a roadmap where whiskey slicked and retrenched
its lines. The next moment, she melts into a cushion
for grandbabies, soft places to lean. The glow she emits is clear

and warm as melted wax. She smells of jasmine or lavender,
depending on the day or place of the sun. But other times,
when the house grows quiet and she thinks no one's looking,

she thins. She becomes paperbag brittle, a hollow with neat,
foldable corners. Her light dims and wavers like flame
caught in a draft. And her hands tremble the air, small circles

working knits and purls, or perhaps scratching the finest
pen tip across a moving page. *Stay still,* she whispers, *stay still.*
It's this sound, nothing or no one hears, that terrifies.

Like a Knife Fraying Rope

My inevitable self acts like she's here to mediate, but we all
know her presence alone shuts down the tug of war between
my other bickering selves like a knife fraying rope. Suddenly

they have nothing left to pull, the war between them slack
and dissipated. *What's the point in worrying about any of this*,
my extraordinary self muses, drying dishes while

my ordinary self washes. From afar they eye my inevitable self
as she strokes the renamed Traitor Cat. They've taken to doing
chores side by side, or going for long walks together, just

to avoid conversation with my older, cantankerous self,
who holds no patience for their drama. She's content
to sit at the kitchen table, watching the coffee in her bowl

shrink away, or listening to the clock's analog tick, each second
spasming into the next. She remains calm always, unmoving
and unmoved. We learn to work around her, a part of the house

taken for granted like foot stools or a knee wall, her function
never stated yet understood by all. Sometimes, she falls asleep
and her snores soften the clock's mechanical twitch. It's then

that Traitor Cat nips her lined, dry finger pads, and she wakes
with a start. *What happened*, she mutters. *What did I miss?*
And then she'll laugh. It's the world's oldest, funniest joke.

Our Decline and Decay

You would think my inevitable self's manifestation
and arrival would terrify my extraordinary self the most,
but my ordinary self feels freaked out beyond repair.

Perhaps because my extraordinary self has already faced,
even welcomed, her own death. My ordinary self
has never considered her own mortality. She looks

at my inevitable self and sees more inefficiency; more
slowness instead of speed; confusion when clarity's required.
Take, for instance, her peculiar fascination with watching

my inevitable self put on socks: The low, slow bend
toward the floor and the groan that issues forth;
her shaking hands grasping for toes, for the intractable

sock mouth and its slippery, horrified O; the rock and sway
as my inevitable self rolls the cotton around her ankles.
At any moment she could topple from the chair and bruise

her face or hip against the cold, hardwood boards.
But she hasn't. Not yet. Although she won't admit it,
my ordinary self waits for that moment, eyes locked

and breath held. She needs to see how close we are to spilling
back into stasis, into earth: our decline and decay simple
gestures, like putting on socks, but repeated every minute.

Every Action Chose This Moment

Yes, my dears, this is all there is, says my inevitable self
to my ordinary and extraordinary selves as we convene
around the breakfast table one Saturday morning after

sleeping late. *This belly, these arms, this divided mind:
this is the sum of extravagant nonsense, the result
of too much time and unused energy, the product of sloth*

*and privilege multiplied over time. We are energies
misdirected.* Outside in the early spring sunshine,
guinea fowl release their impatience into the air,

a roulette wheel's furious spin clacking to a final,
disappointing close. My inevitable self waits until
the sound slows and then claps her hands. *Buck up,*

buttercups, is her reprimand. *Or whatever. Wallow
in your sadness. But your every action chose this
moment. Also, none of it was ever really under*

your control. My ordinary self rolls her eyes and sighs,
begins to clear the dishes. *You make no fucking sense,
old lady,* she says, syrup dripping from her thumb

and tacking the table's surface. My inevitable self
laughs, a notched bark that calls to the guinea fowl,
whose black pinheads scuttle absurd patterns

across the lawn, away from our window. *That's
what I'm saying to you, chicky,* she says with a grin.
If all this philosophy is so much trash, what are you

going to do with it? My ordinary self frowns
and walks away. The knife's slide along porcelain plates,
the excess food's descent and thump into the plastic-

lined metal garbage can, and my inevitable self
sucking her teeth at us all brings the meeting
to its end. We exit in different directions.

The Joke and All Its Implications

For the children, my inevitable self creates stories about
her tattoos and scars. *This one belongs to the time I was drilling*
oil down in the Gulf. I thought it was a shame, all those waters

slick with runoff, so many small birds and fish floating black
and dead in the waves. When we returned to shore, I had Rico—
my guy, I went to him for all my ink—needle their outlines here,

along my arm, a kind of memorial. My youngest daughter
takes her small hands and stretches the bicep skin smooth,
watches the Least Tern's shape extend a long yellow bill

back toward the sky, away from my inevitable self's armpit.
What came next, she asks. The old woman winks at her.
Why, my crew and I saved the world from a meteor. And now

I have this group of stars, exploding, clustered here above my heart.
It turns out my inevitable self is a fan of really bad movies
and Aerosmith lyrics. *Whenever she quotes "Rag Doll,"*

my extraordinary self complains, *part of me dies inside.*
My ordinary self gives a short laugh. *She should have arrived*
much sooner, then. My children hear none of this exchange.

They get the joke and all its implications. *After you stopped*
Armageddon, my boy asks, *what did you do next?* He traces
the curves of a Polish *pisanka*'s faded Easter colors along her shin.

I went back to work. I trained horses out west. My eldest daughter
points to a cactus flower wilted on her wrist. My inevitable self nods,
pulls the flesh around her carpal bones: the bloom opens again.

Wisdom Exacts Its Price

My inevitable self doctors her coffee with whiskey
every morning but abstains from drinking alcohol at night.
Can't sleep for shit if I do, she barks at my ordinary

and extraordinary selves, who have taken to splitting
a bottle of pinot noir most evenings. They watch with eyes
narrowed and mouths pursed with disbelief as she measures

out the bourbon. *You have to use the jigger,* she says. *Try to
freestyle and your day ends before it begins.* My ordinary self
clears her throat and leans toward the mug my inevitable self

has poured her. *The thing is,* she says, *when in this timeline
do we learn such wisdom? How do we get from me*—she points—
to her—and points again—*to you and your bon mots about living?*

Steam rises from the coffee bowls like spirits loosed from graves.
When you learn to shut your mouth and open your eyes and ears.
My inevitable self grins and pats my extraordinary self's

shaking hand. *That's all right,* my elder self says, lifting her cup.
Wisdom comes and exacts its price. You'll see. She closes her eyes
with the first burning sip. She pauses, and drinks again.

Learning Patience

My inevitable self isn't very precious about her body
and where she places it, which means that sometimes
we find her frozen in various parts of the house, waiting

for someone to come to her rescue. Neither my ordinary self
nor my extraordinary self can respect that, but then,
they've never been good at asking for help. Unsurprisingly,

my inevitable self has learned patience, and will wait out
the spasm in her lower back or hang, importuned and limp
as an afghan over the couch arm, until a child or adult

passes by. *Give us a push,* she'll say, or extend an arm for us
to take and pull. One day, we find her trapped in the basement;
for hours we've mistaken the tapping of her cane for water

moving through pipes. *How'd you end up here,* my ordinary self
says, shaking her head with closed eyes to show her deep disdain,
while my extraordinary self navigates between the copper and PVC

to the place where she'll have leverage. My inevitable self laughs
under her breath, thwacks her cane against the oil burner, and ends
my ordinary self's pantomime. *It doesn't matter how I happened here,*

or how you found me, numbnuts. She braces and grunts against
my extraordinary self's assistance. *Instead, ask: what will I do,
what will we do, now that we've found ourselves in this position?*

She extends her arms toward my ordinary self and beckons.
My ordinary self accepts those outstretched hands and pulls,
and, smocked in cobwebs and cricket legs, my inevitable self rises.

Everything More Extreme

My extraordinary self brushes her teeth after
a long day of doing nothing particularly extraordinary,
and finds an ant scaling threads of her hair. It's spring

so they are back again, searching for water, climbing
walls, riding waistbands, pant legs, sleeves, whichever
body part skirts the sink or counter. My extraordinary

self pinches the ant between her fingertips, slides it
from the white wiry rope it climbed and rolls its thorax
and abdomen until it tears in two. My extraordinary self's

breasts ache. She considers: she could be pregnant, but
by the time she spits and watches the white foam swirl
down the drain, she decides it's likely perimenopause.

Lately everything is more extreme, more hyperbolic
than it used to be, and she was always prone to drama.
She studies the lines near her eyes and mouth, the lids

that pucker and sag and betray her lack of hydration.
She considers washing away the day's makeup, but
it fell off hours ago. Smudged mascara loops above

her cheeks. The day's dust feels unearned and also
like a brand burned into her skin. She lifts the water
to her mouth and bathes her teeth and tongue and throat

with its brief, sloppy blessing. Then she closes the tap,
and shuts off the light and fan. Wipes a coarse towel
across her face. Absolute dark pulses all around her.

Shifting and Inscrutable

Finally, my extraordinary self succumbs to the quiet
fear she's felt ever since my inevitable self arrived:
witnessing what we will become, acknowledging daily

what we leave behind. She abandons us, takes
another brief vacation to a faraway city. She brings
our husband, but they move like two fallen tree limbs

surfing river tides, touching incidentally.
He's ghosted by a broken past and haunted
by his own cataract future. So she seeks out

other men, their half-time attention in sports bars,
all the while aware that three seats down, a brunette
twentysomething does it better. In the bar's

mirrored backsplash, she sees all her frayed edges
outlined in neon and washed in the TV's glare.
Outside the bar, the river splits the city with its wet

sinuous body, and by midnight she trips alongside its banks
afloat on champagne and lust. She has never felt more
invented than when she redraws her lipstick, post-coitus,

body sketched with the lines and shades of want.
Her lover is a phone number scratched on paper
she'll leave on the hotel floor. Our husband waits for her

across town, drawing his own face over and over
on cocktail napkins, its outline shifting and inscrutable
as the river outside, and its muddy, littered shore.

Bedlam and Buffoonery

My prodigal extraordinary self returns home, proverbial
tail tucked. Our husband too. Together they've had
a week spent fighting and crying, a time the rest of us find

wasted, except now they both seem calmer, less jittery,
and my extraordinary self claims to love us all, even
my inevitable self, who smiles and pats her hand but

leans back and winks at my ordinary self on the sly,
who then shudders and turns away. It's obvious we're
a cluster-fuck, but how to clean up a mess such as this?

Like a hoarder's house, we're more or less nothing but layers
upon layers of shit. We're a reality TV dream, so much bedlam
and buffoonery: except so banal, so very boring. Look at

my inevitable self pick her nails. My ordinary self extemporizes
about the pros and cons of PTA membership. Again.
And my extraordinary self makes moony eyes at my husband

and then squeezes Traitor Cat until it yowls and bites
her hand. The children avert their eyes and mutter about
homework and video games. My husband grabs another beer.

Goodbye To What Has Been

My husband has routine bloodwork drawn and it's never
been more clear that soon we're going to die, and that maybe
that day is tomorrow, or the next day, or later this afternoon,

in a half hour. First a clot forms at the injection site,
which swells and blooms a beautiful iris color right where
the elbow cradles the vein. Then, after the sonogram

and the doctor's *well, there's nothing much we can do,*
it turns less lovely, a urine stain along the whiter skin
of his inner arm. Within a few days the results are in:

his body really hates him, and with good reason. It might
rebel at any moment in the most gauche, uncouth way:
stroke, heart attack, gallstones, failure of liver function.

Over several beers and last hurrah cheeseburgers we say
goodbye to what has been. At home, my ordinary self
is cleaning the fridge, clearing deli drawers and freezer

shelves of contraband. My extraordinary self stares
wide-eyed at medical horror stories on the internet.
My inevitable self sits in her chair by the open window

and nods, over and over again. Her emphatic *I told you so*
mixes with shrill, riotous birdsong. Our home distends
with this noise and the full, damp, cruel spring air.

Flat Chalk Slates

Because my ordinary self is ordinary, she expects
the standard story structure: conflict, complication,
climax, consequence, conclusion. And of course, a moral,

preferably with pictures. My extraordinary self
looks for vague epiphanies, pseudo-insightful tension
that crests and ends with two people sitting in room:

their large, vacuous silence; the stark cut to black;
the slow creep of final credits. Profundity
you glean days later as you sit and brood in traffic.

A more lyric creature, my inevitable self thinks
narrative is a waste. She says the passing of days,
their story and minutiae, rarely has a point.

She's a weird Sartrean grandmother we mostly ignore,
although, out of everyone, she's probably the most right.
Sometimes a freakout is just a freakout, she insists.

Sometimes, she sighs, *we don't learn a goddamn thing*.
Most of us are flat chalk slates washed clean by time.
Dust and then the darkness. In the end, no lesson remains.

Notes

The poem "Patterns We've Sought" owes a debt to the recurring images in Derek Walcott's collection *White Egrets*.

The poem "The First Real Darkness" nods to T.S. Eliot's "The Love Song of J. Alfred Prufrock."

The last two stanzas in the poem "To Be Present and Enjoy" allude to Ernest Hemingway's short story, "Hills Like White Elephants."

Acknowledgments

Sincere thanks and appreciation to the editors of the following publications for believing in, and publishing, these poems:

Menacing Hedge, Volume 9, Issue 3: "My Heart, Not Hers (And Not Hers Either)," "The First Real Darkness," and "Useless Masks"

Phantom Drift, Volume 10: "A Pendulum's Swing"

Clackamas Literary Review, Volume XXVI: "Learning Patience," "Goodbye to What Has Been," and "Flat Chalk Slates"

Pine Hills Review, August 2023: "Her Terror is Palpable"

Painted Bride Quarterly: "We Want for More," "A Little Push," and "Backseat Scores"

Pine Hills Review, August 9, 2023: "Her Terror is Palpable"

Alice Says Go Fuck Yourself, Issue 1, November 2022: "This is What We Chose," "No Satisfactory Answer," and "Authors of Their Own Sad Ends"

My deepest gratitude to J. Bruce Fuller, Charlie Tobin, PJ Carlisle, and all the staff at Texas Review Press for making such beautiful books and continuing to support my writing.

Heartfelt thanks to Cynthia Marie Hoffman and Sarah Beddow, each of whom offered valuable and useful feedback during the revision of this collection, as well as to my colleagues and dear friends at Suffolk County Community College, especially Michael Boecherer, Colin Clarke, Misty Curreli, Cynthia Eaton, Doug Howard, Adam Penna, Deborah Provenzano, Sandra Sprows, Meredith Starr, L.B. Thompson, and Susan Wood. Thank you for understanding and supporting me vocally when I've needed to protect my writing space. Without your presence of mind, good advice and camaraderie, my teaching career would have overwhelmed me and this book would not have been created.

And much love to the Hunt Lake/Saturday Zoom Poets: Nellie Bridge, Taj Greenlee, Viola Lee, Lucyna Prostko, Rodrigo Rojas, Shradha Shah, and Sara Wallace. Your beautiful poems inspire and challenge me, always.

Finally, to Andrew: Thank you for enduring the to-and-fro of my ambition, offering unequivocal support, being the best traveling companion, and helping me juggle teaching & writing while—against the odds—we maintain this crazy household of kids and dogs. You're still my favorite, and my best.